DRONE ACADEMY

[OPERATION FOXHUNT]

MATTHEW K. MANNING

STONE ARCH BOOKS
a capstone imprint

Drone Academy is published by Stone Arch Books,
a Capstone imprint
1710 Roe Crest Drive
North Mankato, Minnesota 56003
www.mycapstone.com

Library of Congress Cataloging-in-Publication Data is available
on the Library of Congress website.

ISBN: 978-1-4965-6074-2 (library hardcover)
ISBN: 978-1-4965-6078-0 (eBook pdf)

Summary: When Parker Reading, an amateur computer hacker
and member of Drone Academy, learns that a local bank robber
has eluded authorities in her hometown, she begins to hunt
him down, using her computer skills and sleek drone to scan
the streets of her city. But when the thief turns the tables, Parker
goes from being in virtual danger to real-life jeopardy.

Designer: Aruna Rangarajan
Production Specialist: Katy LaVigne

Elements: Shutterstock: Reinke Fox, (drones) design element
throughout, Rost9, (hexagon) Cover, design element,
Supphachai Salaeman, (graphic) Cover, design element
throughout, TRONIN ANDREI, (drones) design element
throughout, WindVector, (video) design element, cover

Printed and bound in Canada.
010790S18

TABLE OF

CONTENTS

ALTITUDE: 1297m   FLIGHT SPEED: 1400km\h

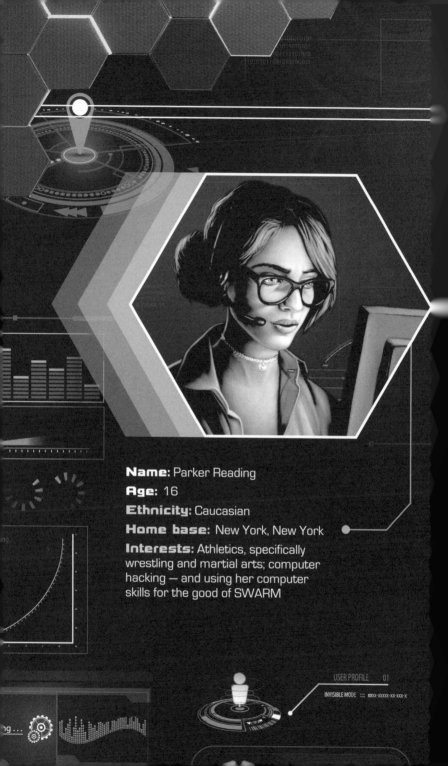

Name: Parker Reading

Age: 16

Ethnicity: Caucasian

Home base: New York, New York

Interests: Athletics, specifically wrestling and martial arts; computer hacking — and using her computer skills for the good of SWARM

ParkourSisters

Drone: Hacker — a small gray drone, almost bug-like in appearance; Hacker has red and green lights and six helicopter blades; the most technologically advanced drone in SWARM's arsenal

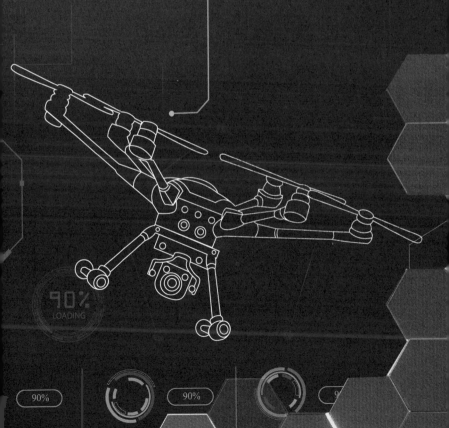

97%

90% LOADING

90%   90%   9

THE SWARM

Society for
Web-Operated
Aerial
Robotic
Missions

HowTo

Name: Howard To

Age: 16

Ethnicity: Vietnamese-American

Home base: Los Angeles, California

Interests: Science fiction, comic books, and all things fantasy — everything from movies starring trolls and elves to role-playing games featuring wizards and warlocks

Drone: Redbird — the sleekest and flashiest of all the SWARM drones; a slick, red hot rod with four black helicopter blades, shiny red paint, red and yellow painted flames on the sides, and a small black camera in its center

TEAM

Zor_elle

Name: Zora Michaels

Age: 16

Ethnicity: African-American

Home base: Rural Indiana

Interests: As far as her classmates know, fashion, trends, and the coolest clothes and accessories; in reality, science, computers, comic books, and SWARM; all things pink

Drone: The Beast — the largest drone on the SWARM team; several feet wide with four industrial gray helicopter blades and a black, crane-like camera; camouflage colors help it blend into its surroundings

saiguy

Name: Sai Patel

Age: 15

Ethnicity: Indian-American

Home base: Savannah, Georgia

Interests: SWARM logo design; a founding member of SWARM

Drone: Solo — the smallest of the SWARM drones; bright white with four blades; a guard bar around the exterior protects those blades while a harness in the center carries Sai's smartphone

CHAPTER 1

FOX IN BOX

Chris Fox wasn't after the money. He knew that was how you got caught. When you saw bank robbers in the movies or on the news, they were always going after the teller's drawer.

"Put the money in the bag!" they'd yell as a shocked bank employee filled their gym bag with a few wads of twenties or hundreds. "And no money off the bottom!"

The last bill in each drawer was supposedly marked so the police could find you. Or it activated a hidden alarm. In some cases, a bundle of bills would contain a dye pack that would turn the robber and the money blue as soon as the stolen loot was opened. It all depended on the story the movie wanted to tell.

Chris wasn't sure if any of that was actually true, but he was not going to risk it. When Chris Fox robbed banks, he avoided the tellers altogether.

That was why, as he walked to the USofA Bank branch on the corner of 5th Avenue and Union Street, it was silent. This section of Brooklyn was dead this time of night, so no one had noticed when he'd pulled the ski mask over his bald head and dark goatee.

It was cold out, and while it was rare, Chris had seen people wearing this kind of thing in the neighborhood before. Worst-case scenario, someone would assume he was a suspicious guy fighting against Brooklyn's icy winter winds.

"You there yet?" an impatient voice asked in Chris's ear.

It was a familiar sound, one Chris had been hearing nearly his entire life. It was Erich, his younger brother, speaking to Chris through the earpiece he wore in his left ear.

"Hold on, hold on," said Chris under his breath.

"I still think you're nuts, hitting a place this close to your home," said Erich. The disapproval was clear in his tone.

"You'll see," Chris whispered in response.

This wasn't the first time Chris's brother had expressed doubts about his intelligence. Sure, Erich was the smart one in the family — at least when it came to electronics and computers. But while Erich had spent practically his entire life locked away in his room, fiddling with motherboards and computer chips, Chris had been learning how the world *really* worked.

And when Chris was sure of a robbery, it meant they could hit it and get away clean. His brother should know that by now.

Chris looked both ways, up and down 5th Avenue. Nothing. The coast was clear.

He placed a metal disc on the door near its handle. The disc adhered to the door's lock, centered perfectly against its keyhole, and let out a gentle whine. A second later, its digital display lit up a bright red. Then it turned green with a sudden click, the display rotating one hundred and eighty degrees.

Just like that, the door was unlocked.

"We're in," said Chris.

"You're welcome," said Erich.

"Cameras?" Chris whispered. The annoyance in his voice was a bit more apparent now.

Erich picked up on it and got to work. A second later, nearly every light inside the bank shut off. The security cameras followed immediately after.

"Done and done," said Erich in his usual chipper voice.

Chris found himself growing more annoyed by the second. He walked over to the locked gate separating him from the small hallway at the back of the bank.

The hall was lined with safe deposit boxes. Hundreds of the silver containers, each secured with two locks. One keyhole belonged to the bank, the other to the customer. Each box required both keys to be turned for the contents to be removed.

But Chris didn't need either. He had his magic silver disc. Erich had built the device six years ago, and it had been a constant source of revenue ever since.

The gate's lock was first. When it clicked open, Chris pushed the gate to the side, walked down the hall, and found box #103. He placed his silver disc on the first keyhole and waited for the light to turn green. Then he did the same with its second keyhole.

With the small metal door unlocked, Chris pulled out the matching metal drawer. He placed it on the center of the table in front of him and reached inside. It was just as the woman in the building next door to his had described to her friend — nearly overflowing with antique jewelry. This box alone was the biggest score of Chris Fox's life.

"Can't keep the lights off too much longer," Erich warned through the earpiece. "Residents are already calling the power company."

"Give me a few minutes," Chris said as he slipped the backpack off his shoulders. He dumped the contents of the box inside and looked again at the wall of safe deposit boxes. "I gotta make this look good."

Chris knew he had to at least empty a dozen or so other boxes if he wanted the robbery to look random and unfocused. He couldn't leave a clue that would lead back to him. Targeting his neighbor's jewelry would certainly be just that.

"You've got ninety seconds," said Erich. "Then the power comes back on."

Chris didn't bother to respond. He was already emptying his third safe deposit box.

CHAPTER 2

FOX IN TALKS

ParkourSisters: *Hey, what's up?*

saiguy: *Not much. Taking Solo out for a test flight.*

ParkourSisters: *Nice! You have any luck adjusting the speed?*

saiguy: *I think so. If it works out, I should get it up to 70mph.*

ParkourSisters: *That's nuts!*

saiguy: *Nah, Boo. That's science.*

saiguy: *You do any more late-night flying recently?*

ParkourSisters: *Yeah. Just had Hacker out buzzing the park and then brought him back. Nothing special.*

ParkourSisters: *He was keeping me company while I crammed for the PSATs.*

"Parker, dinner!" her mom yelled from the next room.

Parker Reading sighed. "Coming!" she yelled back.

She typed a quick goodbye to Sai Patel into the pop-up window on her computer screen. Without waiting for his reply, she stood up from her desk chair.

Parker knew Sai wouldn't be bothered by her abrupt exit. He was used to it by now. That was sort of the way with SWARM — the Society for Web-Operated Aerial Remote Missions.

They were both a part of the group, and Sai knew the habits of its members better than most. He was an avid user of their message boards.

As Parker arched her back, stretching out her muscles, something cracked. Parker cringed. She had spent too much time in front of the computer today. That would change soon enough when wrestling practice started up again. Parker was looking forward to it. She was hoping to best her winning season from last year. After all, the only girl on the wrestling team had to keep up appearances. She was trying to be a trailblazer here. Not to mention it was fun to win — super fun.

As she walked out of her room and down the hall past the bathroom, Parker's feet slipped a bit on the old hardwood floor.

"Whoa!" she said as she nearly fell into the living room.

"Sorry," said her mom. "I mopped when I got home from work. I might have used too much floor polish."

"You think?" said Parker, smiling at a face that looked so similar to her own.

Both Parker and her mother had long blond hair and thin, athletic frames, and both dressed in T-shirts and jeans whenever possible. If it wasn't for the fact that Parker had a good two inches on her mom and her mom had a smattering of freckles and a few wrinkles, they might be mistaken for twins — or sisters at the very least.

Parker's mom found an endless source of joy from people asking if they were sisters. Parker considered it more of an endless source of annoyance. She and her mom were close, but she didn't want to be mistaken for someone who was almost fifty years old. She had a good thirty-four years before she wanted to hear a comment like that.

"I saw that boy again," Mom was saying, "the one with the long hair. He wasn't with anybody, if that's what you're wondering."

"That is not at all what I was wondering," said Parker.

"Why don't you ask him out sometime?" said her mom. "You're very take-charge. He'd probably be impressed."

"I'm not interested in that guy, Mom. Why don't you go ahead and date him if you're so into him?"

"I don't think your father would like that," her mother said with a wry smile.

Parker rolled her eyes. "It's not like he's ever home."

"Parker!"

"Yeah, yeah," Parker muttered. She went to the refrigerator and poured herself a glass of ice water. "I know."

She didn't want to get into that particular conversation again. Her mom defended her dad no matter what. Yeah, he was busy. Yeah, he was a workaholic. Yeah, he paid the insane mortgage on their tiny little Brooklyn apartment. But her mom worked too. And she still found the time to be home and cook dinner every night. She found the time to make it to Parker's wrestling matches and her karate rank tests.

As far as Parker was concerned, Mom never gave herself enough credit. She was too busy talking up Parker's dad. But Dad was a full-grown man. He could talk himself up. If he was ever home, at least.

"Is this about that little friend from the computer?" her mom asked.

"My little friend?"

"What, is he something *more*?"

"I'm part of an online society, Mom," said Parker, sitting in her chair next to the window.

It had been her special spot since she was small enough to fit in a high chair. "It's not a dating site."

"Oh, yes," said her mother, making a sarcastic face. "The all-important SWARM! Very serious business."

"Hey, we found the guy who was stealing from that bodega a few months ago," said Parker.

She understood her mom was just teasing, but it was a sensitive topic. Parker was proud of the work she did with SWARM — or Drone Academy, as she loved calling it. Parker had been one of the founders of this tight-knit online group of teenagers. It was her proudest achievement. Even more so than her black belt in Isshin-Ryu karate and her nearly flawless wrestling record.

"Honey, I'm just pushing your buttons," said her mom.

"And we helped find that family's dog last week. That family in Queens."

"I'm sorry. I shouldn't have teased you."

"We do a lot of good, Mom," Parker said as her mother brought her a white plate with fish, lemon, and a side of asparagus. "And we're getting better every day."

"And I'm sure that boy Howard talks about you as much as you talk about him," Mom said. She shot Parker a wink as she sat down across the table.

"I don't want to talk about Howard," said Parker, turning to look out the window.

"That's a first," Mom said. She cut into her fish. "Did you hear about Mrs. Kingsley?"

"Which one is she again?"

"Parker, you're terrible."

"What?" said Parker, digging into her meal now. "There are a lot of old ladies who live in our building. I can't be expected to keep them all straight."

"She's the lady whose groceries you carry," her mom said. "You do it almost every week."

"Oooh," said Parker. "Betty."

"You're on a first name basis with Mrs. Kingsley?" Mom raised an eyebrow as she sipped her water.

"No," said Parker. "I'm on a first name basis with Betty."

"Sigh."

"You can't say the word *sigh*, Mom," said Parker. She had almost completely devoured her fish already. Her mom was still working on her second bite.

"Well, anyway, there was a robbery a few blocks away, at the USofA Bank," Mom continued, spearing her third bite with her fork. "Mrs. Kingsley's —"

"Betty's."

"Fine . . . *Betty's* safe deposit box was broken into last night. Her entire antique jewelry collection was stolen."

"Oh no!" said Parker. Her voice had changed to one of genuine concern. "She was just telling me about her jewels last week when I was helping her inside. She must have told me that same story a dozen times. She loved that stuff!"

"It sounds like there were about twenty or so boxes broken into. She was one of the unlucky ones."

"Unless she was the target the whole time," Parker said.

"Oh, Parker," Mom said, letting out an actual sigh this time. "Is this going to be another of your *missions*?"

She used air quotes on the last word to get her meaning across. The gesture was not lost on her daughter.

"Gotta go, Mom," Parker said, standing up. She'd already cleaned her plate. She tended to inhale her food. It was worse when she was excited about something. She took her dishes into the kitchen and dropped them in the sink. Then she headed back down the hall toward her room.

"Say hello to Howard for me!" Mom called after her.

Already in her bedroom, Parker rolled her eyes. "Don't think I didn't hear that!"

CHAPTER 3

FOX AND HAWKS

The metal double doors that led to the basement of 4912 Union Street were open again. The doors had been built at an angle, and through them a mess of shadows, an old bicycle, and plenty of storage tubs and boxes were visible.

They were all belongings that the residents of the building above couldn't possibly fit in their small apartments. In some cases, they were things the residents didn't *want* to fit into their small apartments.

But there were a few prized possessions hiding in the basement's dusty corners. There was a model train belonging to Mrs. Monsivais. A baseball card collection Mr. Valente kept hidden from his wife, who tended to throw anything unnecessary into the garbage. There was an aquarium Mr. Donnelly kept telling himself he'd fill up again any day now.

With all those treasures inside, it made sense that the super, Mr. Petit, hated when Parker accidentally left the basement doors open. But when Parker took her drone out for a spin, she thought of little else but getting her bird into the air. Especially at night, when she was tired from a long day and all she wanted to do was relax in front of her computer.

Besides, no matter how much Mr. Petit hated Parker using the communal basement as her drone launch, he hated her old methods even more.

Before being *reassigned* to the basement, Parker had launched her drone right through her bedroom window. It had taken careful planning to get the launch coordinates correct. She'd finally managed but only after banging the drone into the wall a good dozen times, forcing the super to repair the plaster, a window frame, and even a broken window.

The money for the fixes had come from Parker's own pocket, but Mr. Petit still hadn't been happy. He hadn't been even the least bit impressed when Parker finally succeeded in programming her drone to perfectly avoid the window and wall and return to her desk at the press of a single button on her keyboard.

Parker had opted to store her drone in the basement after that, but had kept the shortcut recall button on her keyboard — just in case. Maybe someday she could convince Mr. Petit to let her launch the drone, affectionately named Hacker, from her room again. And if she was honest, maybe she left the basement doors open on purpose a few times, just to show him the merits of launching from her own apartment. So far, Mr. Petit hadn't gotten the hint.

Everyone in Drone Academy — or SWARM, as they all called it — had named his or her drone. Hacker was named after Parker's number-one pastime. When she wasn't in the dojo or on the wrestling mat, she was in front of her computer, learning new skills or applying old ones. Not everything she did was strictly *legal*, but if she was ever going to work for the government's cyber-defense security team, she needed to get her practice hours in any way she could.

Even now, as Parker piloted her drone via a pre-recorded flight pattern, she was busy trying to find a way into the USofA Bank's computer records. She squinted through her dark-framed glasses at the code that took up half her screen. Then she glanced over at Hacker's cam for a second, watching the live-feed camera but not thinking too much about it for the time being.

Hacker hovered high above the traffic circle near Prospect Park, right down the street from the Reading family's apartment. Parker wasn't sure about the legalities of flying a drone in Brooklyn, so she mostly kept her activity to the park and its surrounding areas.

So far it worked. No one seemed to notice the gray, almost bug-like drone. Its green and red flashing lights and six gray helicopter blades didn't draw that much attention. Parker hadn't had any incidents, aside from nearly crashing into a kite or two on a sunny day.

Suddenly, a window popped up on her computer screen.

saiguy: *What's happening?*

ParkourSisters: *Oh, hey. Not much.*

saiguy: *Watching Hacker's GPS signal. Do you ever go anywhere but the park?*

ParkourSisters: *I'm just stretching Hacker's wings. There's something soothing about watching him make rounds when I don't have to pilot.*

saiguy: *The whole point of owning a drone is to fly the thing, Parker.*

ParkourSisters: *Who needs that kind of stress? I just like the view.*

saiguy: *I'm about to take Solo out for a spin. Need my hands free. Switch to audio?*

Parker didn't answer. Instead she pressed a few shortcuts on her keyboard and took her headset out of her desk drawer. She didn't usually *talk* to Sai much. He preferred to instant message whenever possible. From what Parker knew of him — and she knew him pretty well — Sai seemed like the kind of guy who would rather deal with virtual reality than reality itself. Talking on the phone was too much a part of the real world.

"You read me?" Parker said into the black microphone that jutted out of the headset near her cheek.

"Loud and clear," said Sai. "So I know you're hacking right now. That much is obvious."

"I have no idea what you're talking about," Parker said.

"Whenever you zone out like you're doing now, you're hacking," said Sai. "Probably into something you shouldn't be hacking into."

"OK, honesty time?"

"Uh-huh."

"I might have cracked open the USofA Bank's secure server."

"*Formerly* secure server," Sai corrected.

"Yep," said Parker.

"You're not turning to the dark side on us all of a sudden, are you?" asked Sai. "Not that I'd be opposed to a few million in a secret, off-shore account . . ."

"This is serious, Sai," said Parker. "One of my neighbors had her safe deposit box broken into last night. She lost thousands of dollars of jewelry. Maybe more."

"And you're trying to log into the security feed to find out who did it."

"I was," said Parker. "But that's just it — there is no feed. The power was out."

"Somehow, I doubt that was a fluke."

"Yeah, the perp had to be responsible," said Parker. She leaned back in her chair and stole another look at Hacker's live feed. He was still flying over Prospect Park, hovering over a fairly secluded stone pond. Parker liked it there. She had taken her laptop out there more times than she could remember.

"So I guess I should dig up the power company's records and see if I can find anything," Parker said, bringing her mind back to the problem at hand.

"I guess that's the next step," Sai agreed. "The flight cam from last night didn't show anything?"

Parker froze. She had completely forgotten the flight cam. But she didn't want to say that. No way Sai would let that go.

"Did you not have him out last night?" Sai asked after a pause. "Or did you not check the camera feed?" He didn't laugh, but there was certainly amusement in his voice.

Finally, Parker said, "I forgot I had him out, OK? Leave me alone."

Parker always kept Hacker's camera on during flights. She recorded them all and played them back from time to time, sometimes during rough weather when she didn't want to risk taking Hacker outside. That meant there was a recording of last night's flight.

Parker hadn't noticed anything odd while she was studying, but maybe if she was lucky, Hacker had caught the thief on camera near the bank. The way the flight plan was programmed, the drone would have had four, maybe five chances to get the bank in his sights.

"I can't believe you forgot to check your own recording!" Sai said, obviously enjoying himself.

"Yeah, yeah," Parker muttered. She wasn't as amused. "I'm checking now . . ."

Sai didn't respond. He was too busy laughing. Once he got started, he had a hard time stopping. Unfortunately for Parker, Sai would be laughing for quite a while yet.

CHAPTER 4

FOX AND LOCKS

12:47 a.m.

Hacker buzzed slowly over the corner of Union Street and 5th Avenue. As it moved, the drone surveyed the late-night action happening on the street below.

An old woman pushed a shopping cart full of bags and bottles. Two young people out on a date stopped to kiss goodnight on the front stoop of a brownstone. A man in a sanitation worker's uniform limped slowly along, clearly exhausted from a long day's work.

01:47 a.m.

Hacker circled again over Union and 5th. Below, a raccoon popped its head out of a trash can, clutching something shiny in its jaws. A rat scurried across the street, perhaps sensing the drone above, and disappeared under a dumpster, out of sight.

02:47 a.m.

The wind rustled a few stubborn leaves atop a tree planted in a dirt square, surrounded by sidewalk on all sides. There was no other movement.

Just as Hacker changed course and headed back toward Prospect Park, he captured something else — something suspicious. A dark figure was standing by the bank's front door.

The man was in the shot for only three seconds, but he was there. The man was dressed in a long black winter coat and a matching black ski mask.

As Parker watched, the feed captured the man placing some sort of device on the door. After a moment, it seemed to glow.

* * *

ParkourSisters: *There! What is that?*

saiguy: *I don't see anything. That shadow?*

Parker rolled her eyes. She'd already watched the footage several times, but still. She couldn't believe Sai didn't see it.

ParkourSisters: *Are you even looking at this feed? That's a guy. That's clearly a guy.*

saiguy: *OK . . . oh, wait. OK, you're right.*

ParkourSisters: *Thank you!*

saiguy: *So that's him? That's the culprit?*

ParkourSisters: *I think so. Hold on. I'm going to send the footage to the NYPD.*

Minimizing her chat window on the SWARM boards, Parker pulled up a new window and navigated to the NYPD crime stoppers page. She quickly filled out the form, uploaded the footage from Hacker's camera, and hit the submit button.

ParkourSisters: *There. Done. They have to be able to do something with that.*

saiguy: *I don't know what. You can't make out a thing. Just a shadowy guy in a . . . what is that? A ski mask?*

ParkourSisters: *It's gotta be the perp. The police will be able to make out height, maybe weight from this . . .*

saiguy: *There's nothing here. No real way to identify him.*

ParkourSisters: *OK, but see that little glowing disc?*

saiguy: *Yeah . . . oh. I see what you're saying.*

ParkourSisters: *That's our way in. We don't identify the guy. We identify the tech.*

CHAPTER 5

FOX ON WALKS

"So how's the . . . job hunt going?" Erich asked.

Chris had his phone to his ear as he walked down 7th Avenue, heading to his favorite pizza joint. It wasn't a quick walk, but it was well worth it. Fifteen blocks from his apartment was justified when there was good pizza to be had. Quality pizza wasn't as easy to find in New York City as most locals claimed.

Chris had his phone to his ear as he walked. He took a second to smile at the mother pushing a stroller before his face became serious again.

"Not great," said Chris into his phone. "Let's just say he was closed."

"Closed?" Erich said. Chris couldn't see his face, but he knew exactly what expression his brother was making. He'd seen that holier-than-thou look for decades. "Closed for today?"

"Closed forever," said Chris. "We're going to have to find a new guy."

He couldn't say it over the phone, but the *guy* they were referring to was the owner of a pawnshop. Stealing the old lady's jewels was just part of the process. There was still more work to be done. After they stole the jewels, they had to find a place to sell them.

The trick was finding the right pawnshop. They needed a store that could pay them close to what the jewelry was worth, but they also needed a store that didn't ask any questions. They needed a place that was discreet enough to not rat them out if the cops came looking.

Chris had lined up just the place. It was a little corner shop in Queens. He'd used the guy for years now without a hiccup. The man had come highly recommended from another local thief. But now there was a major problem. The police had busted the shop just last week.

If he wanted to do business with his contact, Chris would have to wait five to ten years — that's how long it would take for the guy to get out of jail. Chris couldn't wait that long. He needed to sell the jewels soon, which meant he'd have to start his search all over again.

"So," said Erich. He had clearly taken a moment to calm himself down. "Any leads yet?"

"I'll find something," said Chris. His voice was full of confidence. His mind didn't quite match.

"Keep me posted," said Erich. "I got rent to pay, you know."

"I know."

"Oh, and hey, it might be nothing, but I saw something weird last night."

"Yeah?"

"Yeah. Just a blip."

"That doesn't sound good," Chris said. He stopped outside the pizza place. This was the type of conversation you didn't bring inside with you.

"I was looking at the USofA Bank, digging around in their server, and I noticed someone else," said Erich.

"Someone else? What do you mean *someone else*?"

"Someone else was doing the same thing as me," said Erich. "From the trail he left, it looks like he was poking around the security records."

"So it was a hacker? Is that what you're saying?"

"Yeah," said Erich. "I tried to trace him back to his computer, but he's good. Led me on a couple wild goose chases."

"But he didn't find anything in the records, right? You made sure of that."

"There's no security feed of you to find," Erich assured him. "But I'm still gonna look into this guy. If he's police, we need to know about it."

"OK," said Chris. "Good looking out."

"You just keep hunting for that . . . job, all right?" said Erich. "The sooner we get this stuff gone, the better."

"I'm on it," said Chris. He hung up and dropped the phone into his pocket. Then he pushed open the glass door in front of him. He was on it — but only after a pizza break.

CHAPTER 6

FOX AND CLOCKS

"I know it," said Howard To, smiling at Parker.

Parker smiled back. She liked his smile. He didn't do it as much as he should.

Howard was Vietnamese-American and had dark eyes and hair, a far different look than Parker's light-hued everything. His coloring was just another of his qualities that contrasted with Parker. She was athletic; Howard looked like he hadn't worked out a day in his life.

She was often referred to as peppy; Howard was overly sarcastic. Her heroes were real-life athletes or computer geniuses; Howard's waved swords around or cast magical spells in comic books.

But despite all these differences, Howard — or HowTo, going by his screen name — was Parker's favorite person to talk with.

"So?" said Parker, looking directly at her webcam. "Don't leave me in suspense."

"It's a digital readout display from an iFound timer. It's not something you'd see on a lock-pick device or whatever the heck that is. That's a custom job," Howard said.

"So where would I start looking for something like that?"

"The Internet," said Howard. "That's a really specific, discontinued piece of junk tech. I only know, like, two stores that would even stock it online."

"And you're sending links to those stores to me now?"

Howard playfully rolled his eyes. "No, I'm video chatting with you."

"Well, when you stop gazing into my dreamy eyes you're going to send me those links, right?"

"Geez," said Howard with a grin. "You make it so appealing."

With a wink — Parker had never seen him wink — Howard signed off from their video chat. Less than a minute later, Parker's computer pinged with an email alert.

She opened the email and clicked on the link. As the page loaded, Parker glanced over at Hacker's live feed. The drone was currently flying over 7th Avenue, on his way back to the park. He was almost over that pizza place she liked.

A few minutes later, Parker had successfully found a back door into the first website Howard had sent. She began riffling through the site's digital sales records. Much to her surprise, she came up with a sale for the iFound timer almost immediately. The device had been sent to a post office box in Manhattan.

This could very well be the guy, Parker realized. The digital display hadn't been sent to a personal address. That in and of itself raised a little suspicion.

As Hacker passed over 7th and then 8th Avenues, Parker continued to type. With a little above-board searching, she discovered that the PO Box was registered to a business: E-Rock, Inc. This felt right. Something about this felt like it made sense.

Parker opened a new window on her screen and began to work her magic. The post office in question would have security cameras. It was time to find out if the owner of E-Rock, Inc., wore a black winter jacket.

CHAPTER 7

FOX AND CROCKS

Erich Fox hung up his phone. His brother wasn't answering his calls. That meant one of two things — either Chris had spent the entire day on the subway, or he couldn't find a pawnshop to sell the jewels. Option two seemed more likely.

Chris didn't seem to be taking this setback too seriously. To him, it was a small bump in the road. To Erich, it was different. This was watching a plan, one that had been weeks in the making, fall apart. This was technology *years* in the making being wasted on a heist with no endgame.

Sometimes Erich had a hard time finding common ground with his brother. They were so different. Sure, they were both stubborn. They'd inherited that from their dad. But for years now, Erich had felt like he was doing the lion's share of the work. Chris was the legwork guy. He took the physical risks. But Erich designed all the tech that made their heists possible in the first place. And it was Erich who kept a digital eye on things both before and after each crime.

Erich frowned as he thought about it. Here he was doing all this work, putting in all this effort, and Chris was only there for the hour or so each crime took to commit. Chris kept claiming he was street smart, but what did he really contribute? And now Chris wasn't even answering his calls?

Erich was so lost in thought that he walked right past the post office. When he finally realized his mistake, he stopped, turned around, and walked back toward the old building. It was time to get to work. He popped the collar on his favorite denim jacket, the one with the crocodile logo on the back. Then he headed inside the post office.

It was true, Erich was the real reason for his family's successful criminal activities. But maybe if he possessed the street smarts Chris was always talking about, he might have noticed the gray drone hovering above the lamppost at the corner of the block.

* * *

"There he is!" Parker said into her headset.

"Nice!" said Howard. "So he's the guy you found on the bank's security feed?"

"Yep," said Parker.

"But you don't actually know he's the bank robber yet, right?"

"Well, no," Parker admitted. "But I checked both websites you sent me. He's the only person who ordered that digital display. At least, he was the only person in all of New York, New Jersey, or any of the surrounding states."

"Yeah, it's not a popular piece of tech."

"Lucky for us," Parker said. "I checked the post office's feed, and this guy — the owner of E-Rock, Inc. — comes in every Wednesday about this time. He checks his PO Box and then heads home. Or at least I'm guessing that's where he goes."

"And that's why you have Hacker out today?"

"Yep," said Parker. "Gonna follow this sucker home."

Howard didn't say anything. Parker figured he was looking at the live feed she was sending him on his computer. He was looking for their target, just like she was.

Less than a minute later, the owner of the E-Rock PO Box stepped out of the building, squinted in the sunlight, and turned right to walk back in the direction he'd come from.

For the first time, Parker noticed the green crocodile on the back of the man's denim jacket. It wasn't the black coat from the robbery, that was for sure. But this crocodile man was the only lead she had.

"OK, HowTo, I'm gonna have to lose you," Parker said.

"But we just now found each other in this lifetime," said Howard. It was a cute comment. A bit goofier than something Howard would usually say but cute nonetheless.

"I need my hands free," said Parker. "Clicking off."

"Until we meet again," Howard said in an overly dramatic voice.

Parker didn't respond. The E-Rock guy would get too much of a lead if she wasn't careful. She had just enough time to give Howard a quick laugh before clicking the end button.

CHAPTER 8

FOX DOWN BLOCKS

Parker was careful to keep her distance. She held Hacker half a block back from the man in the crocodile jacket at all times. Using the zoom feature, she kept the camera focused on him and kept the course as steady as she could using her handheld gaming controller rather than her keyboard. For extra safety, she stayed high enough in the air to avoid power lines. Fortunately, she didn't have to worry about the drone being detected due to noise — Hacker wasn't particularly quiet, but neither were New York City streets.

The man in the crocodile jacket turned the corner, and a few seconds later, Hacker turned after him. Parker breathed a sigh of relief when she quickly located her target again. She was lucky he wasn't on to her. If the man started running, she might not be able to keep up.

Parker wasn't the pilot that some of her fellow SWARM members were. Sai had his speed drone and VR goggles. Zora Michaels, the only other female member, had an almost superhuman reaction time and piloting skills that bordered on instinctual. And Howard, he was the most determined out of all of them. He was willing to take chances and make modifications to his drone whenever the situation demanded it. Parker had a hard time understanding why he never bothered to take chances in his personal life.

While Parker was daydreaming about her friends at SWARM, the man in the crocodile jacket had walked several more blocks before turning another corner. Parker got her head back in the game and turned the corner after him, narrowly avoiding a fire escape that had no business being where it was.

She scanned the alleyway below. There was nothing. No man, no reptilian jacket, nothing. Parker felt a tinge of panic travel up her spine. She'd lost him.

Just then there was movement at the very bottom of the screen. Parker panned the camera down slightly and saw a door closing. It was the back entrance to what looked like an apartment complex of some kind.

With the man in the crocodile jacket now safely out of viewing range, Parker lowered Hacker until he was parallel with the door. The closer inspection revealed the number 21 on the door. This wasn't an entrance to an entire apartment building — it was the way into one particular basement apartment.

If this man was the culprit, Parker had just discovered his home address. And the best news was, the suspect had no idea that anyone was on his tail.

Parker smiled as she typed in the command for Hacker to return to his charging base in her building's basement. Then she opened a new chat window. She had to tell Howard the good news.

* * *

Erich Fox continued to look out of his apartment's peephole. The drone that had been following him for blocks had grown bolder. Erich had noticed its green and red lights and gray spinning blades a few blocks after he'd left the post office. The drone was now hovering right outside, its camera pointed right at his door. He wondered if it could see through his peephole.

Before he could think too much about it, the drone swiveled, rose into the air, and flew out of sight. It was probably heading home — or worse, Erich thought, it could be hovering above the building, waiting for him to leave again.

Erich stood completely still, letting his fear slowly transform into pure rage. Then in a huff, he stormed over to his computer and powered it on.

CHAPTER 9

FOX AND JOCKS

Parker was exhausted. Karate class had gone long, and it was a sparring night. Sparring nights were always harder than kata nights. No matter how many times or at what speed Parker practiced her katas, they were still just a pre-arranged set of kicks, punches, and stances. They weren't the cardio workout that sparring was.

Parker sighed as she dried her hair in the bathroom. She was happy to have washed off the hour's worth of sweat, but she could already feel new beads forming on her forehead in the hot bathroom. Even her lightweight sweatpants and her old white T-shirt felt too hot.

As Parker exited the room, she nearly collided with her mother. Mom was busy putting a diamond earring in one ear and attempting to put a high-heeled shoe on one foot at the same time.

Luckily, despite every part of her body aching, Parker still managed to dodge her mom. She sidestepped out of the way in time to avoid a collision.

"Hey now!" Parker said.

"Sorry, sugar," said her mom. "I'm already late meeting your father."

"I could have sworn you two had already met," said Parker. She was never too tired for one-liners.

"Good night," Parker said.

"Night, Parker," Mom said. And then as quickly as she had appeared, her mother was gone.

Parker peered down the dimly lit hallway of her apartment building. The super had time to complain about her drone, but no time to change a light bulb once in a while?

Parker shut the door and flipped the top and bottom locks. Then she walked over to the kitchen and pulled a boxed pizza out of the freezer. Nothing like a healthy dinner to complement a healthy workout.

She slid the pizza out of its packaging and then into the oven, not bothering to preheat it. After setting the oven to three hundred and fifty degrees, Parker walked back down the hallway to her room, a fresh glass of water in hand. Time to see what the SWARM gang was up to.

* * *

"You sure you got the address right?" Chris said into his phone. He shivered as he walked down the street. It was colder outside than he had anticipated.

"Yeah, I'm sure," said Erich. "Some of us are good at our jobs."

"Pfft," Chris said, dismissing his brother's comment. "So this guy, you think he got us on film?"

"The night of the —?" Erich started to say when Chris interrupted.

"Cell phones, remember," Chris warned his brother. "Let's keep the details to a minimum."

"The night of the . . . incident?" Erich said instead. "I don't know. All I can think is that maybe he somehow got me on camera leaving the post office. That's the first time I noticed the drone. And that's the PO Box I used when I ordered all of the parts to make the . . . device."

"So tell me again how you found him," said Chris.

"I've already told you three times," said Erich.

"Pretend I'm as stupid as you think I am."

Erich sighed. Then finally, he said, "It took some doing, but I tracked his IP address back through the bank's website. He was digging around in the security camera files."

"Right."

"Once I had that, I looked into some feeds nearby — an ATM camera on the corner, the security camera outside the apartment next door. That's how I spotted the drone. The same one that was following me outside the post office."

"I just don't get how this guy lives so close to me," Chris said into the phone.

"I told you we shouldn't have hit a place right around the corner from where you live," said Erich.

"Cell phones," Chris said again, noticeably more annoyed this time.

"All right, take a look in front of you, Mr. High Security," Erich said.

Chris did. From his position on the sidewalk he could see two rusted doors at the bottom of the building. They led down to the basement of 4912 Union Street, two buildings down from his own.

"At least there's easy access," said Erich.

"I'm going in," said Chris. "Cell phone silence until I call you in an hour. Somebody's gotta clean up your mess."

"*My* mess?" Erich said.

But he was wasting his breath. Chris had already hung up.

CHAPTER 10

FOX WHO STALKS

Parker finally made it to her desk chair, but it took a Herculean effort. Every one of her muscles ached. Even her brain felt like mush. She needed sleep, but Parker was a night owl. She was sure a second wind was coming.

On her desk sat a smoldering, formerly frozen pizza. Parker picked up a slice and bit into it, instantly regretting not waiting. It was still way too hot. Now her gums were on the list of body parts that hurt.

Without getting up, Parker managed to lean over and open her window, hoping the light from her computer screen and small desk lamp wouldn't attract any moths or other flying critters. She had removed her window screen months ago to accommodate Hacker, and hadn't bothered to replace it. The rest of her lights were off, though, so hopefully she wouldn't have to deal with any unannounced visitors.

The computer made its triumphant loading sound, and Parker began to pay attention to it. She logged into the SWARM website to see who else was online tonight. At the same time, she opened her drone navigation program. She had made sure the basement doors were open tonight on her way home from karate. Hacker had been waiting patiently for her go command ever since.

Surprisingly, no one was on the SWARM site. Parker had been hoping to talk to Sai or Howard about the case. Now that Hacker was freshly charged, she planned to take him back into New York City. She'd set up a stakeout outside the apartment of the crocodile man and would hopefully catch him heading somewhere.

Tailing him had been more fun than Parker had originally thought. Now if only she could catch him in the act of something illegal. If she was really lucky, maybe he would try to sell the jewels he had stolen. No matter what he did, Parker would have some new information on him. And information was the most valuable commodity.

Parker had already typed the man's address into Hacker's programming. He would fly to that destination using his map navigation feature, giving Parker some free time to do a little sleuthing of her own. She and Hacker were becoming a better team every day. It was the perfect working relationship — he did the legwork, and she did the thinking.

* * *

Chris Fox was trying not to think about his brother as he made his way through the dark basement of 4912 Union Street. His mind was focused on the job at hand. He was going to find the other hacker. He wasn't sure what he was going to do when he found him, but it wasn't going to be pretty.

As Chris placed one foot on the bottom of the wooden staircase that led up to the building's first floor, something moved in the corner of his eye. He snapped his head to the side just in time to see red and green lights flashing in some sort of bizarre sequence. Then there was the sound of fan blades and the hum of something that sounded like a motor.

None of it made any sense until the shadowy thing lifted into the air. It was the drone Erich had tracked. But it wasn't moving toward Chris — it was heading for the double doors. A moment later, the drone flew out of the basement.

After the thing was gone, Chris let out a sigh of relief. He'd debated shutting the doors but hadn't wanted to draw any attention to himself. Apparently that had been exactly the right call.

Putting his mind back to the task in front of him, Chris continued up the stairs. Erich had said the apartment he was looking for was 3B.

* * *

Parker jumped when she heard the sound at the front door. Then she calmed herself. It was just the doorknob. Mom and Dad were probably back early.

She headed out of her bedroom and walked down the hall toward the door. All the while, the doorknob rattled.

Did they forget their keys? Parker wondered. *I thought Mom grabbed hers when she left.*

She was nearly at the door when she heard a low electronic whine. It wasn't a noise Parker had ever heard before. She looked out the peephole, but she didn't see her mother's face smiling back at her or her father fumbling for his keychain. She saw a man with a shaved head, a goatee, and . . . a black coat.

Parker did her best to hold her gasp in as she stepped away from the door. She'd been so busy tracking the bank robber, she hadn't even considered the possibility that *he* was capable of tracking *her*.

As she stood there, there was a sickening *click* from the door. It had unlocked itself, as easily as if the man on the other side had a key. The electronic whine sounded again. He was working on the bolt lock now.

Parker wanted to run. She wanted to scream. She wanted to grab her phone from her desk and call the police. But instead, she was frozen in place. She felt like she couldn't move. This was what all those years of martial-arts training had gotten her.

She was a deer in the headlights — and the man in the coat was an oncoming truck.

CHAPTER 11

FOX HITS ROCKS

"Do you need help, young man?" said a woman in the hallway.

Chris turned around to see someone much older than he expected. She had gray hair and glasses so thick they couldn't possibly do her any good. "No, ma'am," he said, practicing his kindest smile. "I'm good. Just having trouble with the lock."

"Are you a friend of the Readings?" the woman asked.

Chris did his best to maintain his smile. Apparently he was in the middle of a conversation now.

"Oh, wait," she said. "I know you. You live in the building two doors down."

Chris had no idea what to say. This wasn't a good development.

"I think you have me confused with someone else," he finally replied. "I'm staying with the Readings this week." Despite the lie, his voice seemed calm. He sounded natural and authentic.

"Oh," said the old woman. "You're probably right, then. My eyesight isn't what it used to be."

"Whose is?" Chris said.

The woman smiled at the thought. "You have a nice night now," she said as she shuffled past him. "Don't let those tricky locks get the better of you."

"I'll do my best, ma'am," Chris said. He continued to smile at her until she had made her way down the hall and turned the corner to the stairwell. It seemed to take hours.

Once she was out of sight, Chris turned back to the door. He placed the disc above the bolt lock again and watched it glow.

* * *

Hearing the conversation through the door hadn't calmed Parker's nerves. But when she heard the lock click open, enough was enough. She finally unfroze. There was no time to waste.

Moving as quickly and silently as she could, Parker sprinted down the hallway and into her room. She had her door closed and locked by the time the front door opened behind her.

Now all she had to do was come up with a plan.

CHAPTER 12

FOX GETS CLOCKED

Chris Fox walked into the apartment. He didn't bother to say anything. He didn't yell down the hall to see if anyone was home. He wanted whatever element of surprise he could muster.

He looked in the kitchen and at the small eating nook next to it. The lights were all off. There was no one there. Chris continued in. No one in the living room. No one in the dark hallway. He moved to the bathroom and flipped the light switch. Again, it was empty.

There were two other doors down the hall, likely leading to bedrooms. But Chris was looking for a master hacker, and it wasn't that late. His brother had said this man kept crazy hours. If he was home, surely he'd still be awake.

Chris swung open the door on the left first. It was as dark as the rest of the apartment. He switched on the lights. There was a king-size bed in the center of the room. There was a dresser and a lounge chair but no people.

Chris paused when he noticed the small nightstand next to the bed. There was a photo on it. In the picture stood a man, presumably his wife, and a daughter.

This master hacker was a family man, Chris realized. It made what he had to do all the more difficult. But the hacker had brought this on himself. He'd poked his digital head where it didn't belong.

Shutting the door behind him, Chris reached across the hallway and gripped the other bedroom's doorknob. It was locked. He tried it again, but it didn't budge.

Chris was about to reach for the silver disc in his coat pocket when he heard a sound from the other side of the door. It was a small noise, no more than the shuffling of feet. But there was no doubt about it, Chris was not alone in this apartment.

The break-in had taken much too long already. He couldn't afford to waste another second. The person behind the door probably already called the cops. The hacker knew he was here.

Chris braced himself and rammed the door with his shoulder. It collapsed inward more easily than he had expected. He nearly lost his balance as he stumbled into the room. A second later, something collided with his face.

It took Chris a few seconds to notice the searing pain. He touched his fingers to his nose and looked down at his hand. There was blood. Someone had just punched him.

His eyes adjusted, focusing on the small person standing squarely in front of him. It was a blond girl, a high schooler at best. There she stood, her fists raised like a prize fighter.

Chris was so stunned that it took him a second to process what had happened. Had the hacker escaped? This coward had left his teenage daughter to fend for herself? What a scumbag.

But when he looked from the girl to the computer situated on her desk the truth hit him, almost as hard as her fist had. There was a live aerial feed running. Another pop-up box displayed computer code.

Chris looked at the girl again. *"You?"* he said. "You're the hacker?"

"No," the girl said, looking over at her window. "He's over there."

* * *

As Parker watched, the intruder moved toward the window she had pointed to. It led out onto a fire escape. Parker froze in place, still in her fighting position, and held her breath. She had no idea if her timing would work.

At exactly that moment, Hacker came home. The recall program was still operational. The drone navigated his way perfectly through Parker's window, avoiding the wall and glass, just as she'd programmed him. But Hacker didn't avoid the head of the man standing in Parker's apartment.

Just as suddenly as he had broken down her door, the intruder was lying on Parker's floor, unconscious, with a half-broken drone resting on his face.

CHAPTER 13

FOX IN STOCKS

saiguy: *I don't believe you.*

ParkourSisters: *It's true. It happened.*

saiguy: *You can keep saying that, but I still won't believe you. How long?*

ParkourSisters: *Ten minutes.*

saiguy: *You Skyped with Zora for ten full minutes?*

ParkourSisters: *At least.*

saiguy: *Man, you are just full of wins this week.*

ParkourSisters: *To be fair, she was at a coffee shop. She still doesn't want me making fun of her way-too-pink bedroom.*

saiguy: *So how's the aftermath now that you put the notorious Fox brothers in the clink?*

ParkourSisters: *Normal people don't say the word* clink *in real life.*

saiguy: *I'm not normal people.*

ParkourSisters: *You can say that again. Things are good. It took some quick thinking to explain how Chris Fox found me, and Mom says she's never letting me out of her sight again. But I haven't had too much to worry about since the cops followed my anonymous tip and caught Erich Fox on that train headed for Connecticut.*

saiguy: *You impress me, Parker. And I don't impress easily.*

ParkourSisters: *That's funny. Zora said the same thing.*

"Parker!" Mom shouted from down the hall. "Hurry up!"

That was the third time she'd yelled already. If Parker didn't answer her soon, she was afraid her mom would panic and break down her newly repaired bedroom door.

"Coming, Mom!" she called. She signed off with Sai and was about to shut down her computer when the machine pinged again. She looked at the screen. Howard was IM'ing her.

"Honey," Parker's mom said as she cracked open the door and stuck her head through. "Your father's outside in the car. He's double parked, and we have dinner reservations in fifteen minutes."

"I'm coming," said Parker. She tried to make eye contact with her mom, but Mom was looking at Parker's computer screen instead.

"Is that Howard?"

"Moooom," Parker said, rolling her eyes as hard as humanly possible.

"You know what," Mom said, "I'm going to tell your father to drive around the block a few times. You two have your little chat."

"He can't even hear you, and I'm completely embarrassed," Parker called as her mom left the room.

But as she typed on her keyboard, Parker was smiling.

* * *

It had taken only two weeks for the new inmate to get to know the guard stationed at the far end of the prison yard. As it turned out, they were both from the same neighborhood . . . or at least that's how the inmate told it.

He would keep chatting with the guard every day or so from now on. Soon, he'd feel comfortable enough with the man to bring up the possibility of the guard delivering him a package. The inmate would bide his time and locate the least complicated lock on the fence of the yard. And after a few bribes, he would have his silver disc in his hand once more.

No matter what, the inmate would give no indication of his plan. He was too smart for that. After all, Chris Fox knew that was how you got caught.

ABOUT THE AUTHOR

The author of the Amazon best-selling hardcover *Batman: A Visual History*, Matthew K. Manning has contributed to many comic books, including *Beware the Batman, Spider-Man Unlimited, Pirates of the Caribbean: Six Sea Shanties, Justice League Adventures, Looney Tunes, and Scooby-Doo, Where Are You?* When not writing comics themselves, Manning often authors books about comics, as well as a series of young reader books starring Superman, Batman, and the Flash for Capstone. He currently resides in Asheville, North Carolina, with his wife, Dorothy, and their two daughters, Lillian and Gwendolyn. Visit him online at www.matthewkmanning.com.

GLOSSARY

aerial [AIR-ee-uhl] — relating to aircraft

bodega [boh-DEY-guh] — a small grocery store in an urban area, usually one specializing in Hispanic groceries

culprit [KUHL-prit] — one accused of or guilty of a crime or a fault

drone [drohn] — an aircraft or ship without a pilot that is controlled by radio signals

mortgage [MAWR-gij] — a transfer of rights to a piece of property, usually a house, in return for a loan; it is canceled when the loan is paid

pawnshop [PAWN-shop] — the shop of a pawnbroker, especially one where stolen items are displayed and sold

secluded [si-KLOO-did] — hidden from view

server [SUR-ver] — a computer in a network that is used to provide services, such as access to shared files or the routing of email, to other computers in the network

wry [rhy] — cleverly humorous or expressing irony

DISCUSSION QUESTIONS

1 Why do you think Parker's mom gives her a hard time about her involvement in Drone Academy? Talk about some possible reasons.

2 Chris Fox seemed surprised to learn Parker was the hacker. Why do you think that was? Talk about who he expected the hacker to be versus what turned out to be true.

3 Do you think Parker's plan to stop the bank robbers was safe? Talk about some other ways she could have helped.

WRITING PROMPTS

1 Imagine you are a member
of SWARM. Write a paragraph
describing your drone. What
would it look like, and what
characteristics would it have?

2 The Fox brothers have a
complicated relationship. Write
a paragraph about your relationship
with a sibling or other close relative.

3 Write a paragraph describing
Parker and Howard's relationship.
Are they just friends or
something more?

READ ALL THE OTHER DRONE ACADEMY MISSIONS

Despite being a founding member of Drone Academy, **Zora Michaels** is viewed as a flighty girly-girl by her fellow high schoolers. Little do they know, Zora's real passion lies behind her keyboard. But when the younger brother of a classmate goes missing, during a forest fire no less, it's up to Zora to use her drone to locate and rescue the runaway, all while keeping her identity a secret from her increasingly nosy peers.

Sai Patel takes every opportunity to stand up for underdogs being cyber-bullied. But Sai's life takes a dramatic turn when a nemesis customizes a drone to look exactly like Sai's, using it to commit theft, interrupt emergency rescues, and cause as much trouble as possible. Now Sai must prove his innocence using his own drone to bring its doppelgänger to justice.

Howard To has always been on the geeky side, but there's one girl who brings him out of his shell — unfortunately, she's Hollywood's hottest sci-fi star and way out of Howard's league. But when the starlet is hounded by a stalker who uses a drone to spy on her private life, Howard employs his own drone to engage in aerial combat with the stalker's UAV.